# This book belongs to

_____

_____

*For Conrad*

E. D.

This edition published by Albury Books in 2016
Albury Court, Albury, Thame, OX9 2LP, United Kingdom

Text © Mark Marshall • Illustrations © Mark Marshall
The rights of Mark Marshall to be identified as the author and
illustrator have been asserted by them in accordance with the
Copyright, Designs and Patents Act, 1988

ISBN 978-1-910235-44-7
(paperback)

A CIP catalogue record for this book is available from the
British Library 10 9 8 7 6 5 4 3
Printed in China

# Best Bear

Emma
Dodd

Albury Children's

Day's end,
time for bed.
Cuddle up
best Ted.

Worn fur,
kissed away.
Was white
now grey.

Button eye,
patchwork nose,
places where
stuffing shows.

Old bear,
many mends.
We are
best friends.

Toys, toys everywhere. Only one special bear!

All alone, dark night.
Snuggle down, squeeze tight.

What's that
by the door?
Shapes loom.
Hold your paw.

Any monsters
don't dare,
come near
MY bear.

You're brave,
me too.
Scared of the dark?
Not with you!

Safe, sound, warm, cosy.
Start to feel a little dozy.

Wonder what tomorrow brings?
Lots and lots of lovely things.

Night's here,
sleep time.
I'm yours
you're mine!